You can achieve anything you set your mind to just stay humble.

J&J

1

THE MIGHTY

GABOR

The following story, while based on myth, legend, and religion, is in no way meant to be treated as dogma by readers. It is a tale of fantasy simply meant to be read and enjoyed by all.

WHOOOSH

click

THUD
Twas an unfair match... By the sons of Abraham, I have never been so humiliated!
Come now, Baran, we must count our blessings. At least we lasted five minutes longer than last time
Pompous oaf! He does know this be a team, correct?
Gabor, thou art amazing!
Gabor! We love yee! Gabor!
Do you believe this to be my greatest victory? Thou art wrong! For yonder morning, shall come a new challenge: a beast thrice as colossal!
THE NEXT DAY
THE DAY AFTER
THE DAY AFTER
THE DAY AFTER

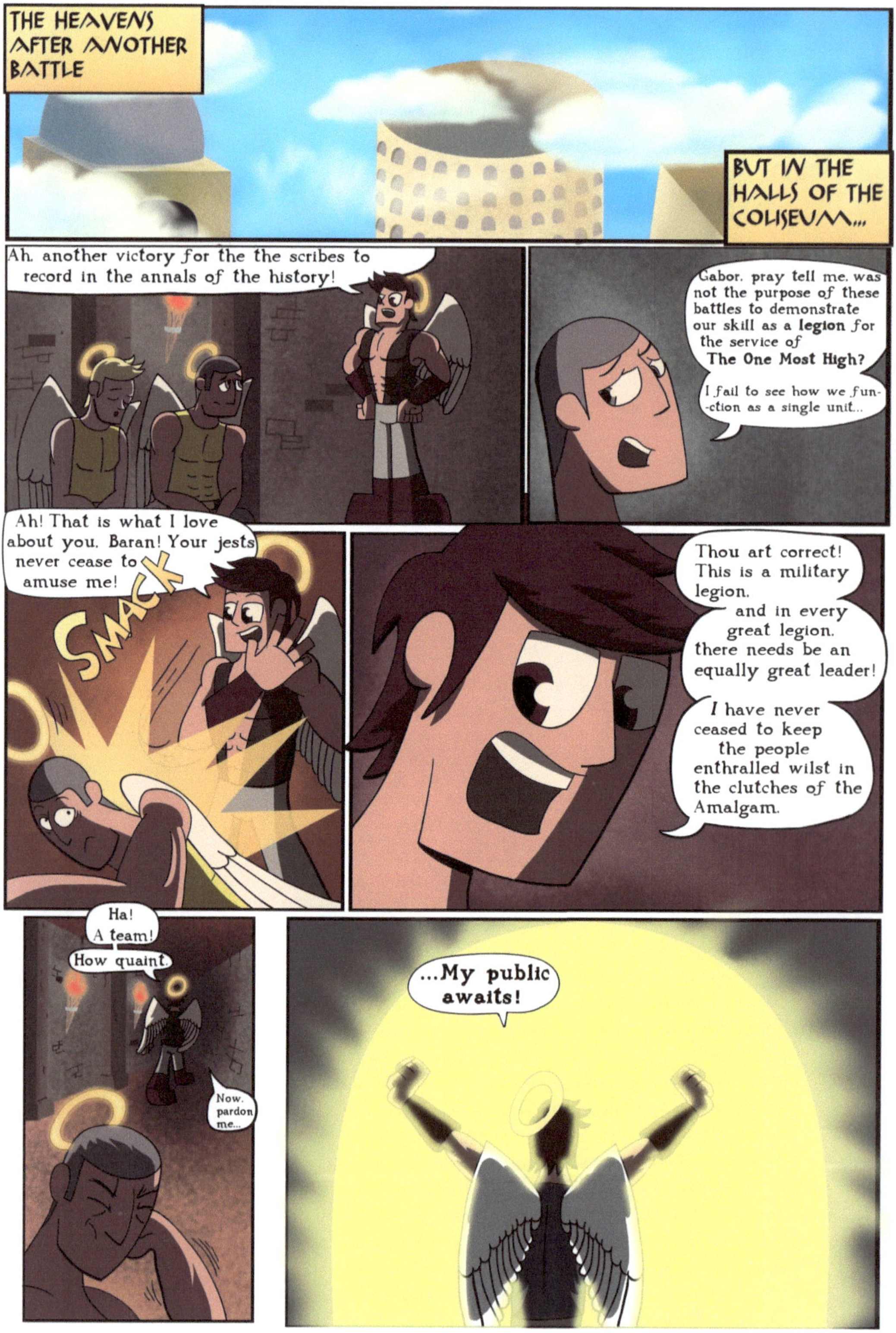

THE HEAVENS AFTER ANOTHER BATTLE

BUT IN THE HALLS OF THE COLISEUM...

Ah, another victory for the the scribes to record in the annals of the history!

Gabor, pray tell me, was not the purpose of these battles to demonstrate our skill as a **legion** for the service of **The One Most High?**

I fail to see how we function as a single unit...

Ah! That is what I love about you, Baran! Your jests never cease to amuse me!

SMACK

Thou art correct! This is a military legion,

and in every great legion, there needs be an equally great leader!

I have never ceased to keep the people enthralled wilst in the clutches of the Amalgam.

Gabor! Acknowledge my craftsmanship!

Ahh! We love yee! Thou art marvelous!

Gabor! This is such an honour! I...
Always a pleasure!

Pardon me!
I doth wish to speak to the hero of the hour.

I am the scribe for the fellowship of the followers of Gabor.
Umm. woulds't thee mind enlightening the fellowship with the secret of thine success?
Hard work.
plenty of practice.
and of course...
Admirable followers such as **thee.**
I pray thee all. thank you for thy ceaseless admiration.
Yet. now ...
I must bid you...
Adieu!

RUMBLE
RUMBLE
Philos!

Thou hast startled me, old friend!
Thou must be hungry.
Let us prepare our meal!
CHOP
want some?
huh.
a team...

SMASH
BAM

Gabor son of Gamliel! Come hither at once!
I hath spoken with thy Commander. Thou hast not aided thy comrades in the arena —to their detriment.
The glory of battle has filled your heart with pride,
and I should have you know that there is no room for **pride** in **this realm!**
Fine, Ariadne. If it doth satisfy thee.
I shall aid those fools and curb my success.
Thou hast one fortnight to heed my counsel.
ON THE WAY HOME
So, shall you heed her advice?
Will you fight alongside your brothers in arms?
Grr...
Listen. I far outclass those hapless fools.
What would that old hag do? Ban me from the stadiums? I wouldst be gone for less than a week before my adoring public demands my return.
ONE FORTNIGHT LATER...

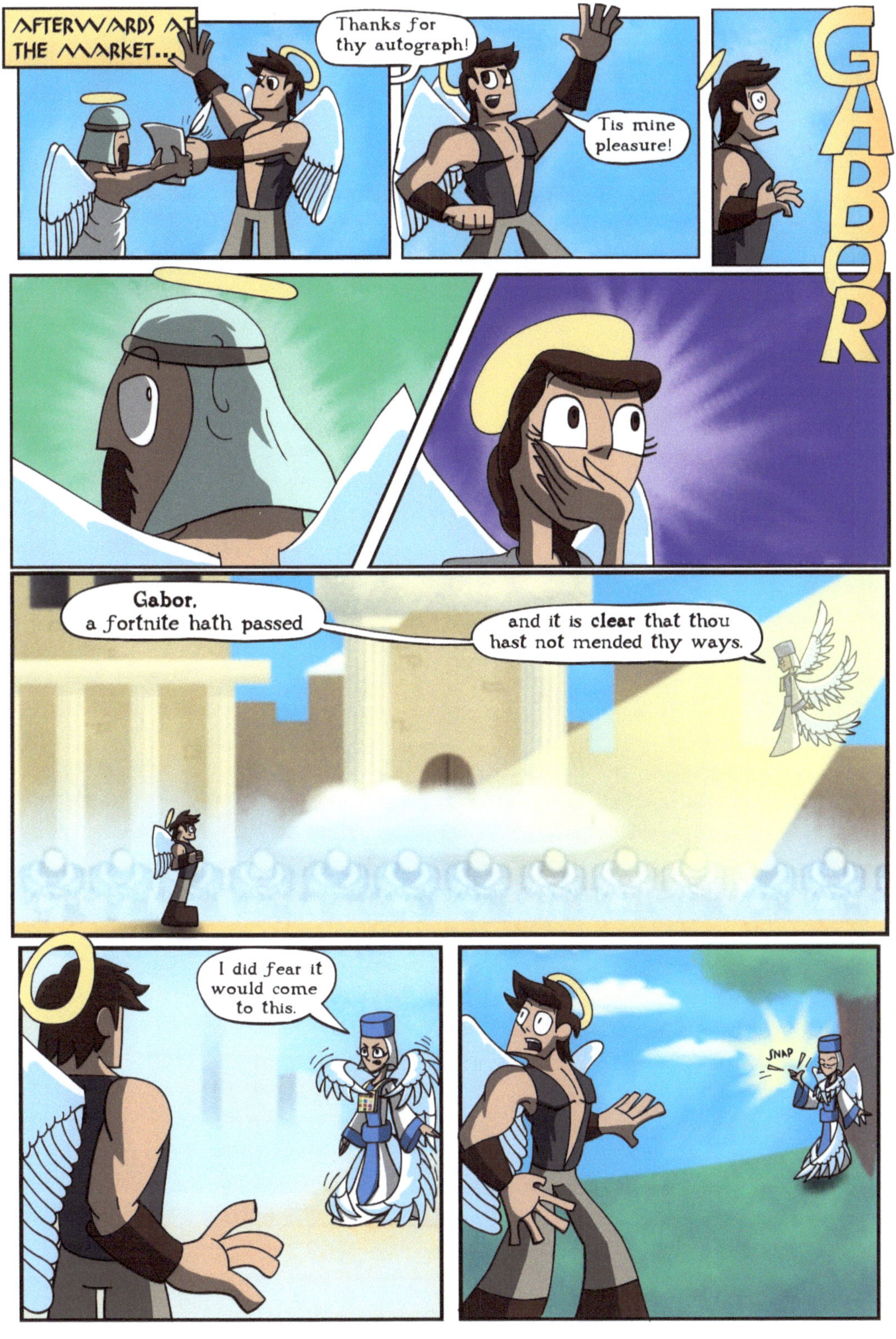

AFTERWARDS AT THE MARKET...

Thanks for thy autograph!

Tis mine pleasure!

GABOR

Gabor, a fortnite hath passed

and it is **clear** that thou hast not mended thy ways.

Thy arrogance and disobedience, Gabor, I shall no longer tolerate.
Thou doth not know how it pains me to deliver thine sentence.
Spare me thy lecture! I hath risen far beyond my brethren in both skill and strength
no opponent hath prevailed against **me!**
For I am **the** mightiest warrior in **all the heavens!!**
Your tongue...
...Speaks...
BLASPHEMY!
!
WHAM

By my authority as a member of the High Nabi of heaven...
...under the Power and service of The One Most High.
I relinquish thee of thine wings!
THUD
I hereby decree thee banished from the heavens. Gabor son of Gamliel!
TO BE CONTINUED...

J&J

2

THE MIGHTY

GABOR

Created by: Jack Harping & J Nanney

THUD!

Egh

Ariadne!
She hath taken my wings!
Why, when I doth...
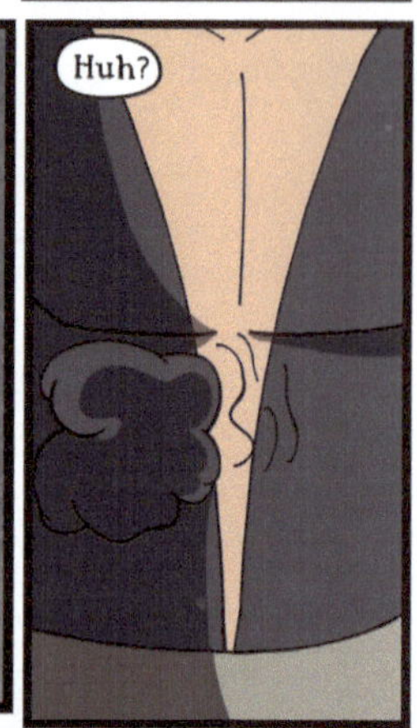
Huh?

Philos! How hath—?!
...well, at least I doth have some company.

Now...
...where art we?

Greetings. might ye...

...

Pardon me, what doth..?

huh?
ZOOOOM

RUMBLE
RUMBLE
RUMBLE
RUMBLE RUMBLE
RUMBLE
RUMBLE
RUMBLE RUMBLE
Wha-!?

SIP

Wow...

Hmm. I doth believe I am beginning to understand.
These poor creatures see me as some sort of champion.

Ah, finally, a people who recognize a great warrior!
I'll simply fight this serpent, and thus they shall worship me as their hero.

Behold, all ye here! I shall slay this beast, and return unto you victorious!

THUD
GULP

CHOMP

SMASH

WHAM
No!
No! No!
No! No No!
NOOOOOOOOOOOOOOO!
TO BE CONTINUED...

J&J
3
THE MIGHTY
GABOR

RUMBLE

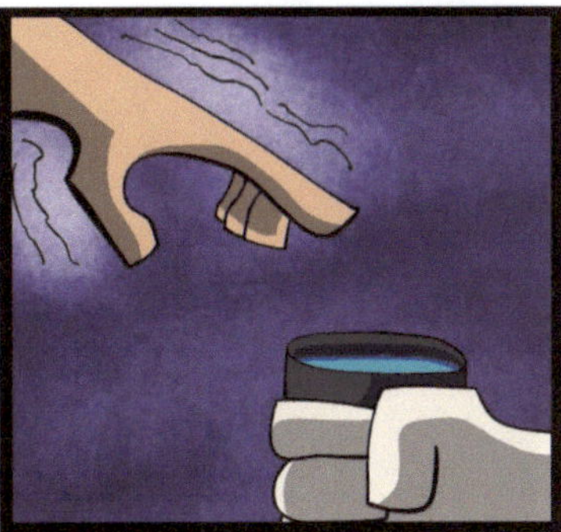

THUD

...

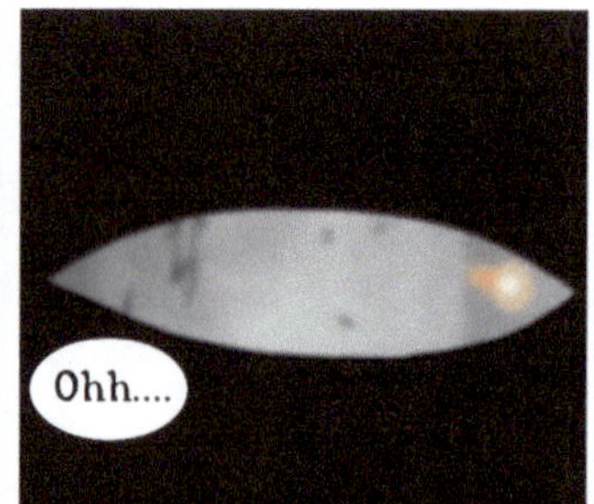
Ohh....

What-?

Well...the mighty savior returns...
By the Great Pillar of Fire!
Thou doth speaketh my tongue?

To dwell within a cavern for one's entire life...
...one finds they have much time for reading scrolls of ancient dialects.

So...light-bringer....
um...my name is Gabor

Ah, Gabor.
I am the chief of this village, and for three generations, we have been trapped below the surface.
The serpent abstructs the sole way out.
So, for returning so wounded, did you at least defeat the serpent?

...the beast was... mightier than anticipated.
I see...

Here, garb yourself, Gabor.

I must give you a proper tour of our home.
Come with me.

These are the people of my village. We may be small in number...
...yet we continue to scrape out a living through farming the moss that grows in the caves...
...and drinking from the spring of fresh water.

Wha—?

Philos! Bad Millinix!

...

mmm...

Thanks
sniff
Sniff

No!

BOOM

What in the heavens was that?!
Those, my friend, are But in your tongue, they would be called "Boom Shrooms."

Look around you. We are not warriors. We are farmers, craftsmen, and merchants.
So, Gabor, I beg you
—will you train us to fight, so that we may prevail over this beast together and find salvation?
FRUMP

Verily, my friend. We shall succeed.

OVER THE NEXT FEW DAYS

CRACK

TUG

Hear Ye!
Thou must heed my words most carefully.
A sure aim is key to our victory. I wilt toss my halo fifteen cubits. and whosoever shall pierce the center. shall be chosen as chief marksman.

FFINK

Congratulations.
Rabab!
Thou shallt be our lead archer.

I think we art ready.

LATER THAT NIGHT
My fellow brothers and sisters of the underground, this is a most glorious occasion: the eve of our liberation. Tomorrow, our mettle shall be tested, and to survive, we must hold firm.

Whatever happens tomorrow, let us give honor to the one who has prepared us.

Drip Drip

WHILE THE VILLAGERS SLEEP
I give you my thanks, Gabor,

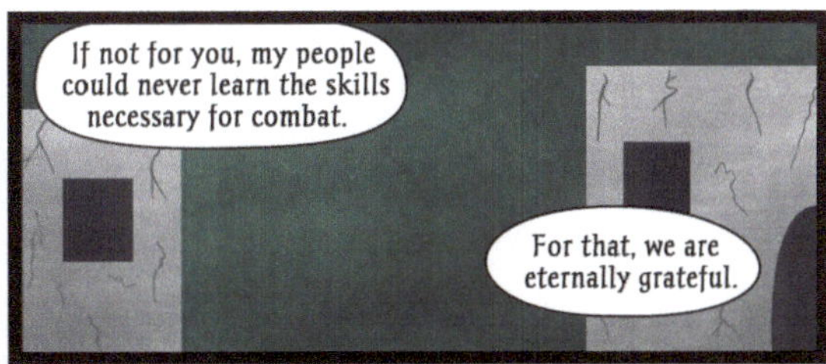
If not for you, my people could never learn the skills necessary for combat.
For that, we are eternally grateful.

But, Gabor, heed these words:
If we do not succeed against the creature, we cannot return to the village...

...for the water is gone.

I understand.

Verily it is true my friend. When I first discovered the prophecy.
I **thought** I could single-handedly vanquish the creature with all the bravado of an undefeated gladiator.
Yet in my failure. I did realize the limit of my strength. Truly it is the **people of this village** and their safety that matters most...
...And that is why I **bequeath** to you...

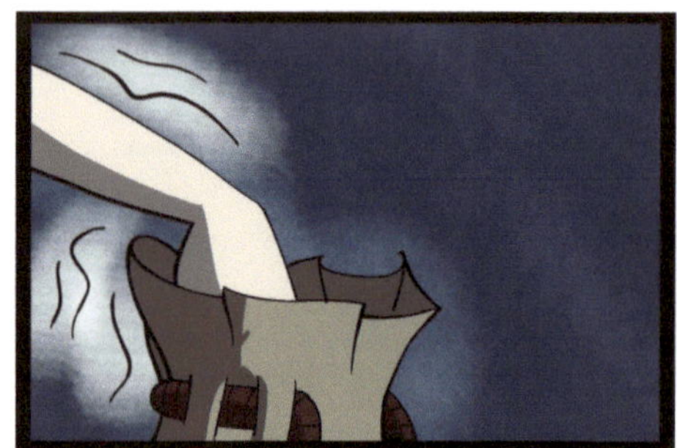

The mushrooms?

Why?

When fighting the creature, I did spy these volatile fungi lining its cave.
If anything were to go awry...

Do not fret my friend.

You have trained these men well.
TO BE CONTINUED...

J&J
4
THE MIGHTY
GABOR
This ends. NOW!

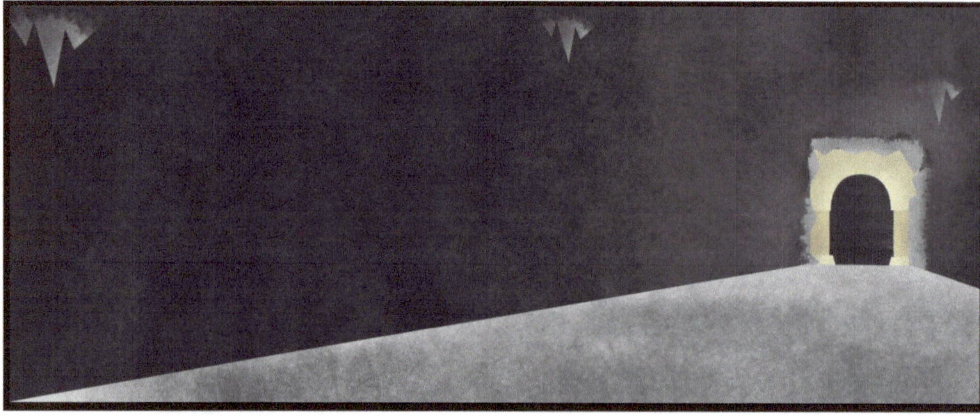

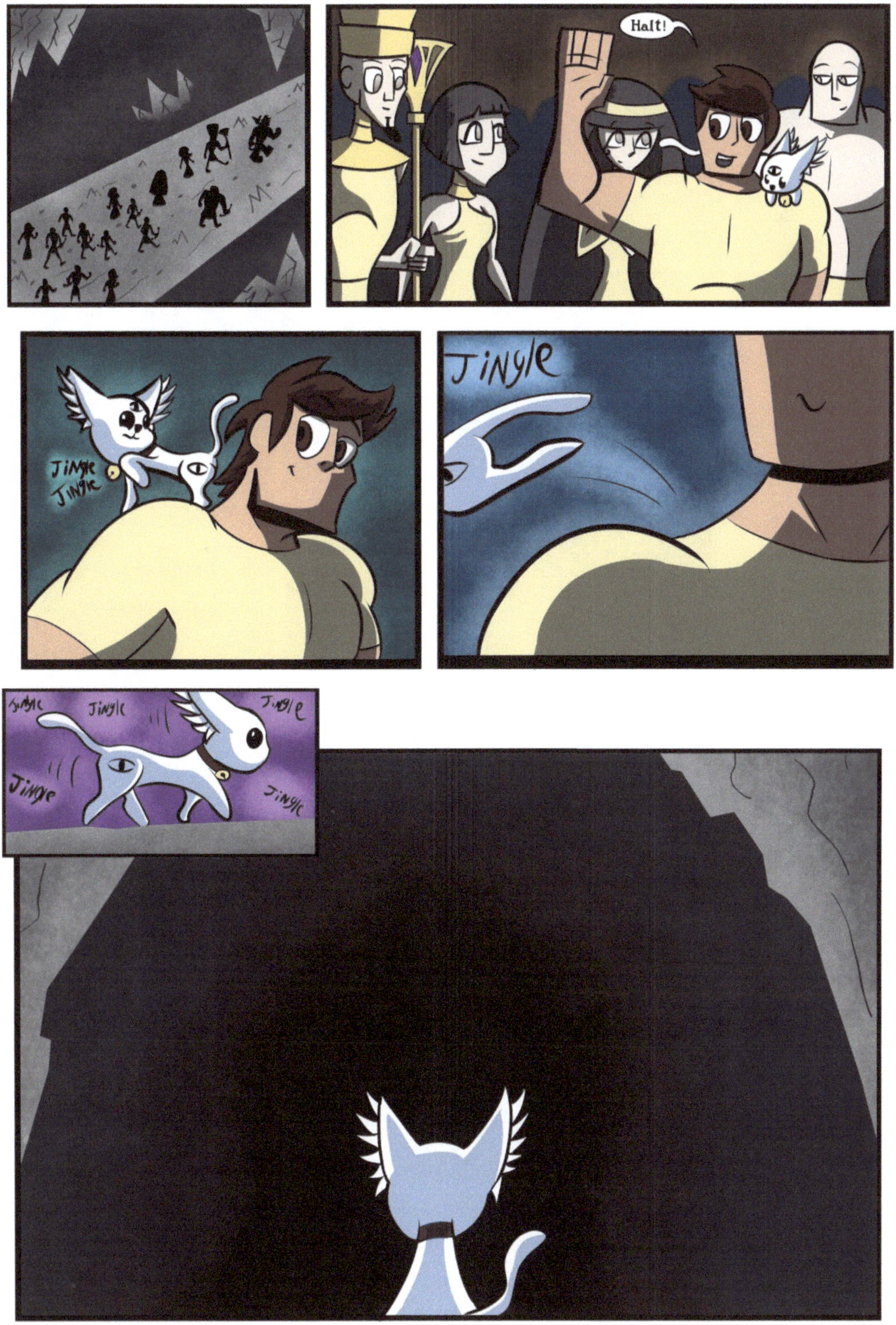

Jingle
Jingle
Jingle
Jingle
Jingle

GULP!

CRUNCH
Jingle

DINK

WHAM!

Now!
Over the foul creature!

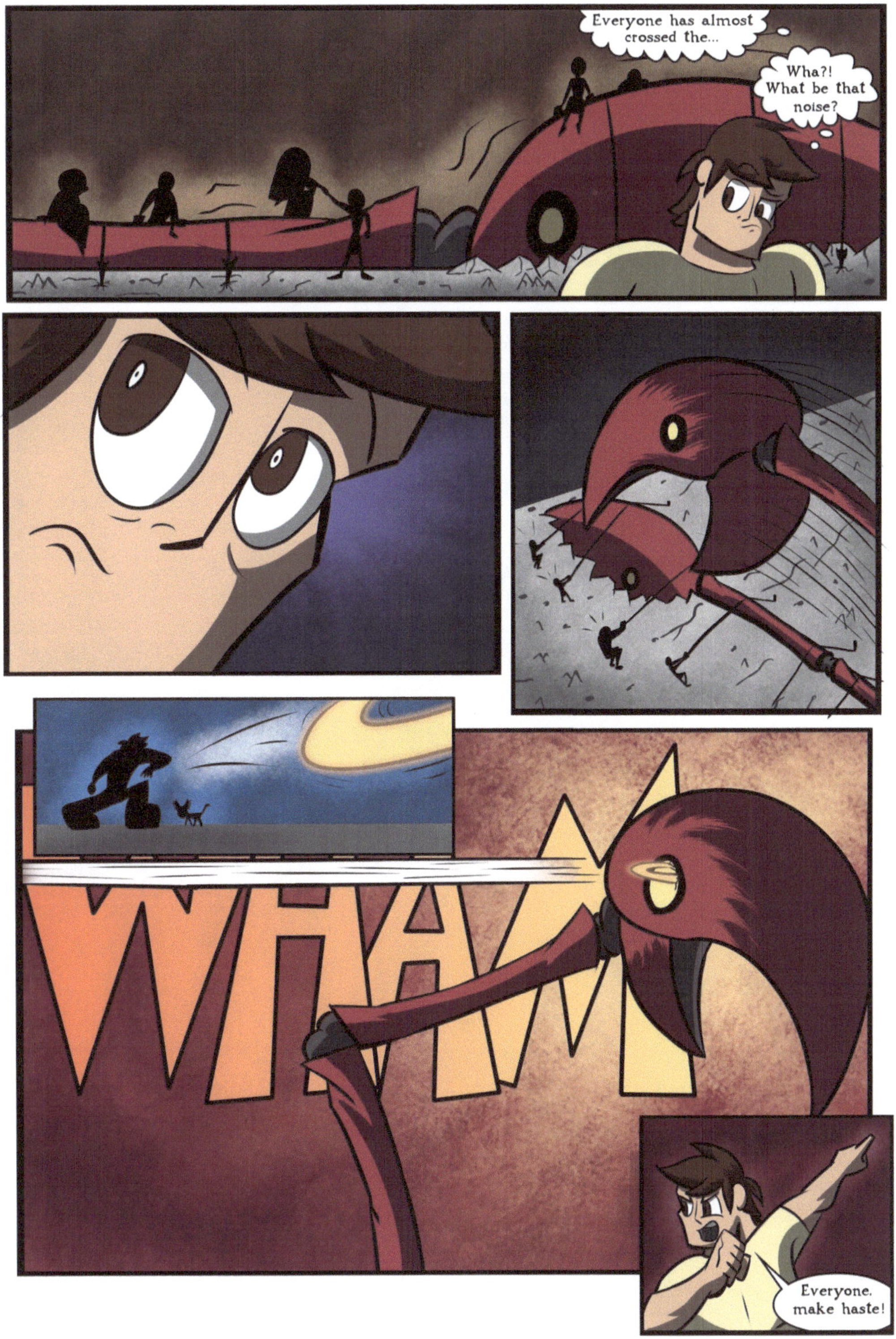

WHAM

Everyone, make haste!

Go on! Not one soul shall be abandoned this day!

PLINK

RUMBLE

RR
RRUUUUUUUN
BBBBLLLLE

BOOM

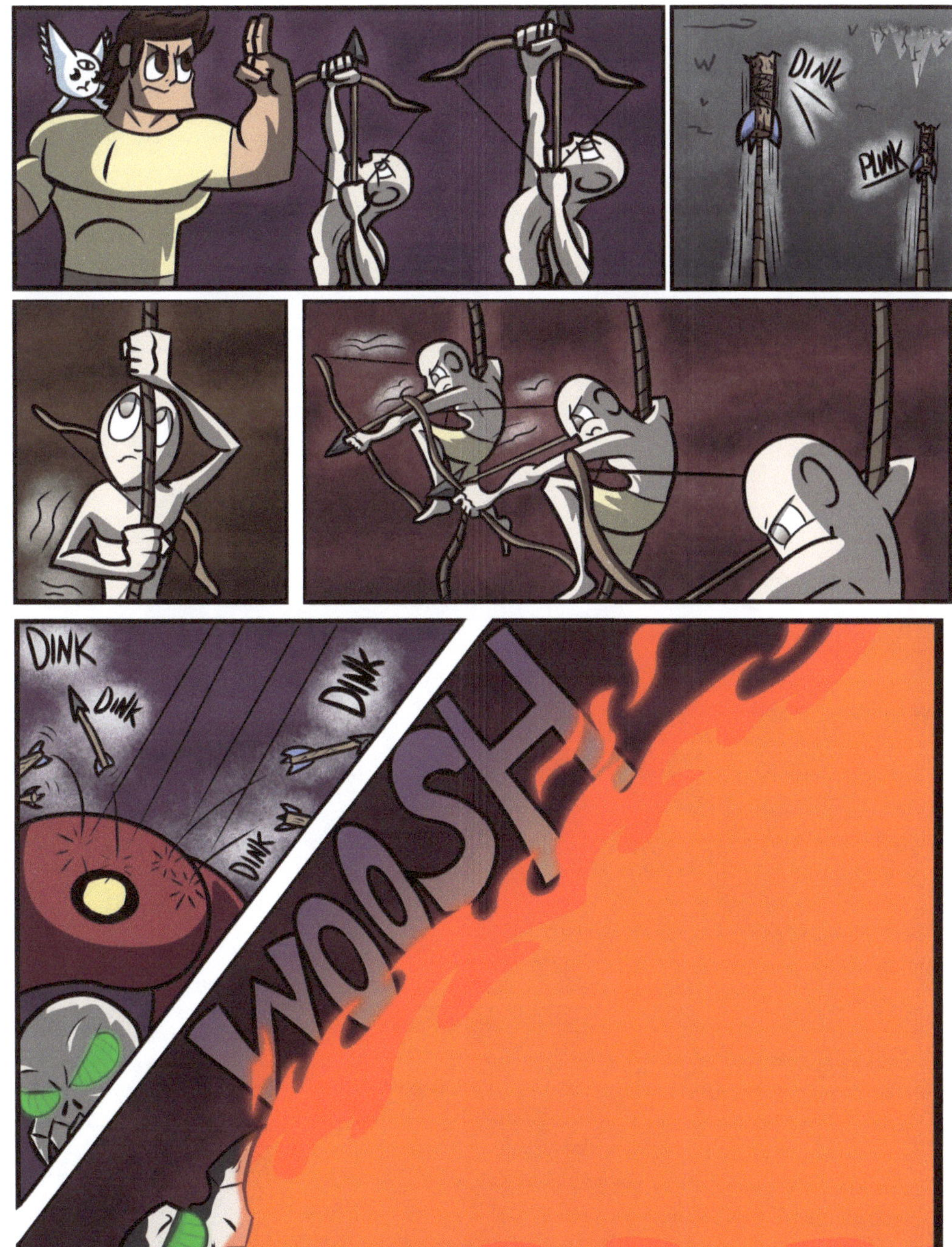

DINK
PLINK
DINK
DINK
DINK
DINK
WOOSH

PLOP

Lead the villagers to the surface!
I will distract the foul beast and buy thee some time!

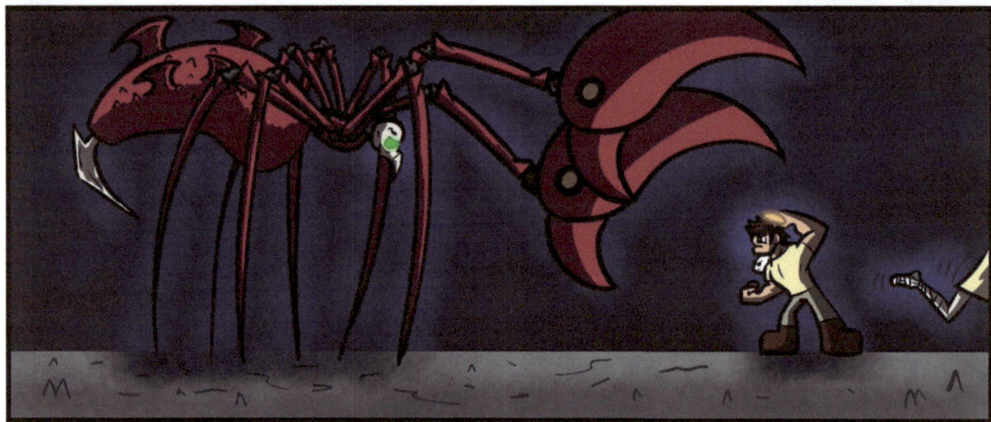

WHAM

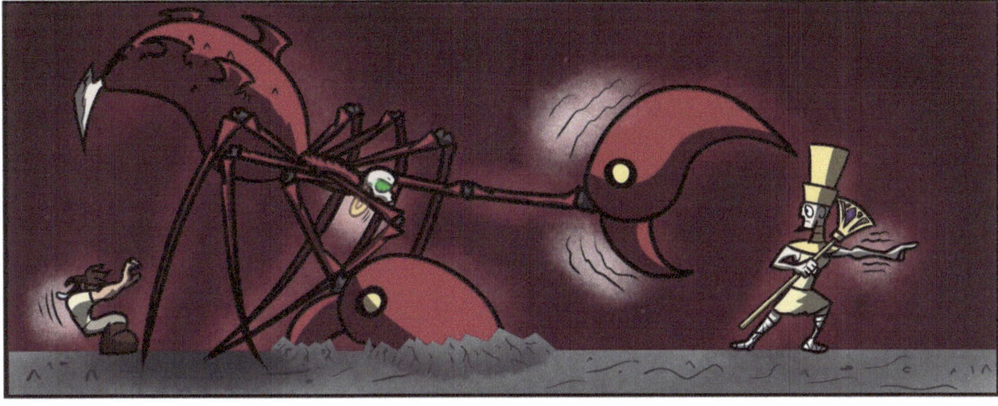

GGGGRRRRRRRA

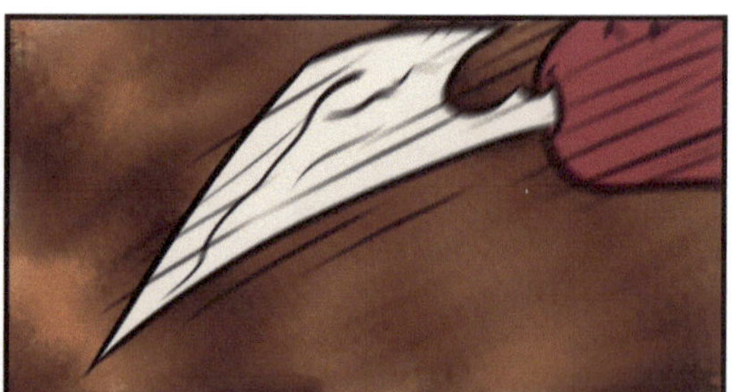

BAM

BAM

CRUNCH

POKE POKE

Gabor!

Hurry, Gabor! We have made it outside!

You must come quickly!

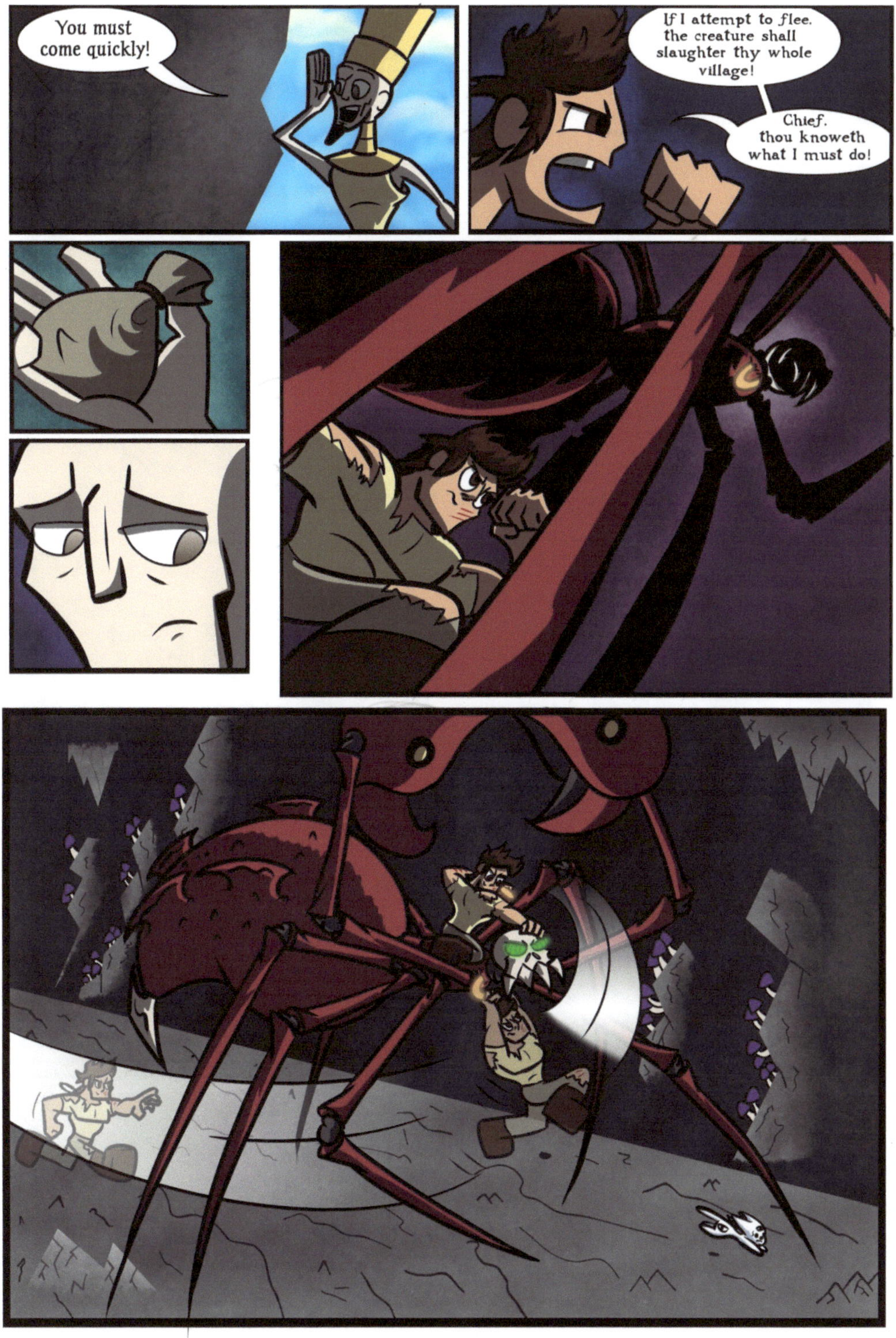

If I attempt to flee, the creature shall slaughter thy whole village!
Chief, thou knoweth what I must do!

BAM

Use it! It must **not** escape!

WHAM

CHOMP

Farewell, Gabor! We shall never forget what you've done.

BOOOOM

Rumble
Rumble

RUMBLE

RUMBLE

CRUNCH

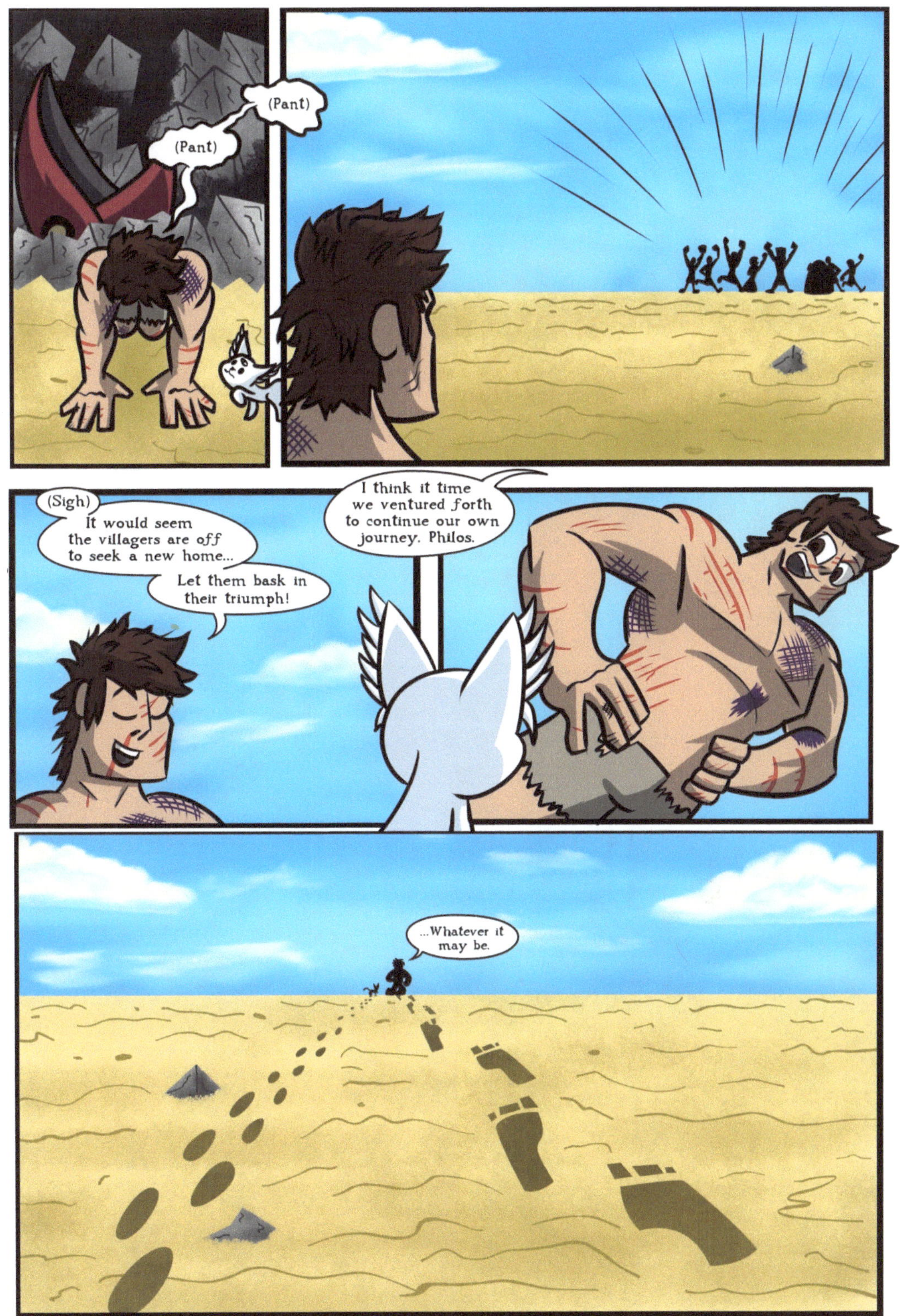

(Pant)
(Pant)
(Sigh)
It would seem the villagers are off to seek a new home...
Let them bask in their triumph!
I think it time we ventured forth to continue our own journey. Philos.
...Whatever it may be.

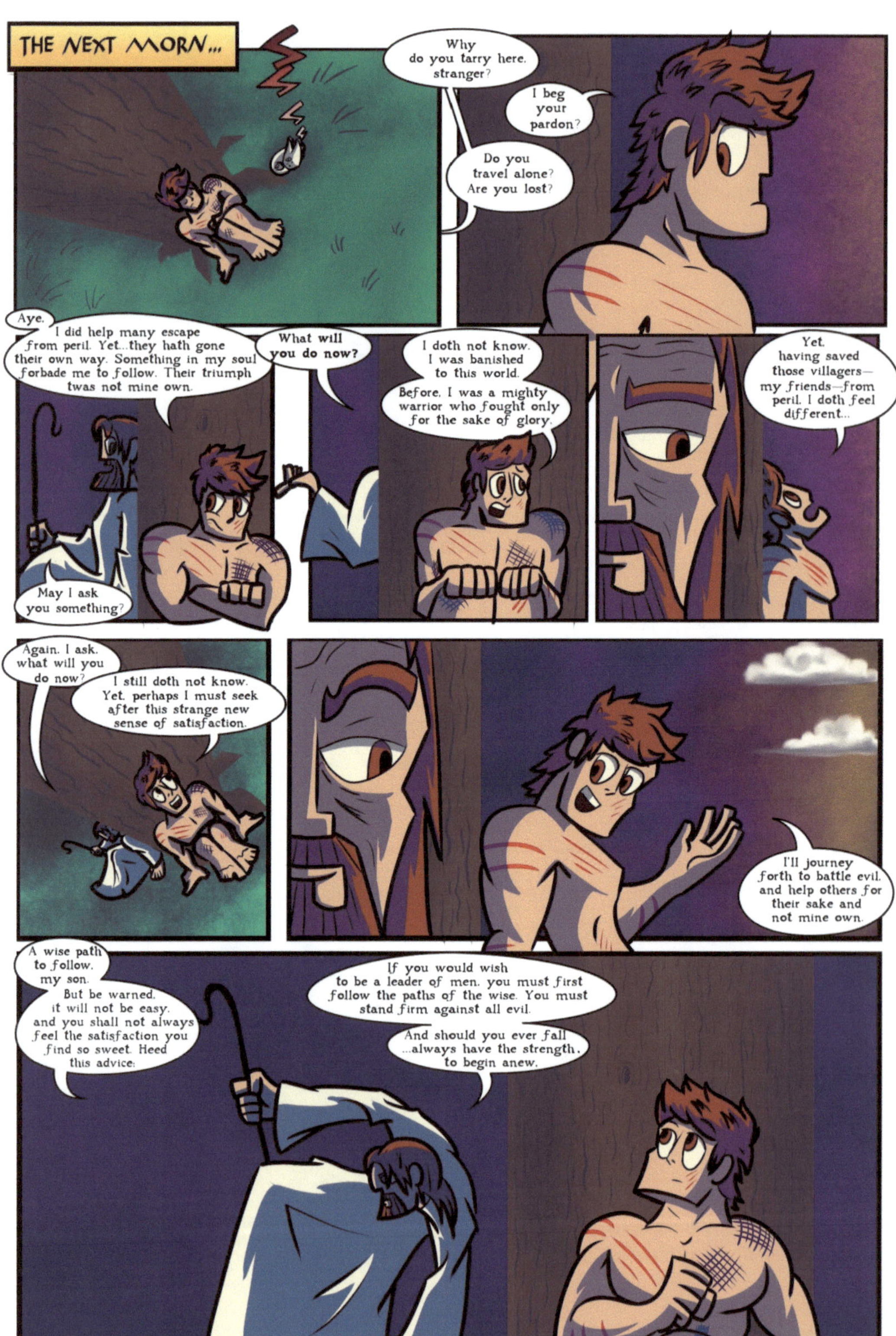THE NEXT MORN...
Why do you tarry here, stranger?
I beg your pardon?
Do you travel alone? Are you lost?
Aye. I did help many escape from peril. Yet...they hath gone their own way. Something in my soul forbade me to follow. Their triumph twas not mine own.
May I ask you something?
What will you do now?
I doth not know. I was banished to this world.
Before, I was a mighty warrior who fought only for the sake of glory.
Yet, having saved those villagers—my friends—from peril, I doth feel different...
Again, I ask, what will you do now?
I still doth not know. Yet, perhaps I must seek after this strange new sense of satisfaction.
I'll journey forth to battle evil, and help others for their sake and not mine own.
A wise path to follow, my son.
But be warned, it will not be easy, and you shall not always feel the satisfaction you find so sweet. Heed this advice:
If you would wish to be a leader of men, you must first follow the paths of the wise. You must stand firm against all evil.
And should you ever fall ...always have the strength, to begin anew.

Arise, my son...
...your time has come.

Now go forth
have no fear.
Spread thy
wings and fly.

THE END?

Early Designs

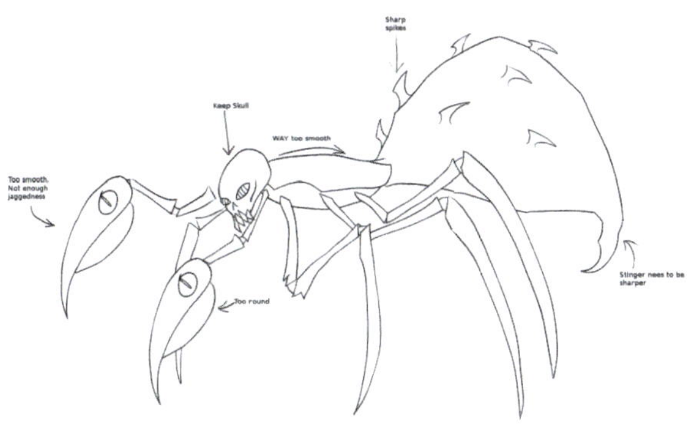
Sharp spikes
Keep Skull
WAY too smooth
Too smooth. Not enough jaggedness
Too round
Stinger nees to be sharper

Concept art

www.ingramcontent.com/pod-product-compliance
Lightning Source LLC
LaVergne TN
LVHW052258100826
845147LV00001B/77